Hickory Dickory Dock!
The mouse ran up the clock!
The clock struck one,
The mouse ran down,
Hickory Dickory Dock!

Hickory Dickory Dock!
The cat climbed up the clock!
The clock struck two,
The cat said 'meow',
Hickory Dickory Dock!

Hicko.. Dickory Dock

illustrated by Kelly Caswell

Child's Play (International) Ltd
Ashworth Rd, Bridgemead, Swindon, SN5 7YD UK
Swindon   Auburn ME   Sydney
                                     China

Is the clock going to chime?
Who's going first?
It's a long way up!
Race you to the top!
Ready, Steady, Go!

Hickory Dickory Dock!
The snake slid up the clock!
The clock struck three,
The rat jumped free,
Hickory Dickory Dock!

Hickory Dickory Dock!
The crab crawled up the clock!
The clock struck four,
The crab snapped its claw,
Hickory Dickory Dock!

Hickory Dickory Dock!
The bee buzzed up the clock!
The clock struck five,
The bee hid in its hive,
Hickory Dickory Dock!

Hickory Dickory Dock!
The dog dashed up the clock!
The clock struck six,
The dog did tricks,
Hickory Dickory Dock!

Hickory Dickory Dock!
The lamb leapt up the clock!
The clock struck seven,
The lamb lay in its pen,
Hickory Dickory Dock!

Hickory Dickory Dock!
The frog hopped up the clock!
The clock struck eight,
The frog jumped the gate,
Hickory Dickory Dock!

Hickory Dickory Dock!
The skunk slunk up the clock!
The clock struck nine,
The skunk smelt fine,
Hickory Dickory Dock!

Hickory Dickory Dock!
The bear bounced up the clock!
The clock struck ten,
The bear bounced again,
Hickory Dickory Dock!

Hickory Dickory Dock!
The worm squirmed up the clock!
The clock struck eleven,
The worm squirmed again,
Hickory Dickory Dock!

Hickory Dickory Dock!
The rat raced up the clock!
The clock struck twelve,
The rat hid on a shelf,
Hickory Dickory Dock!

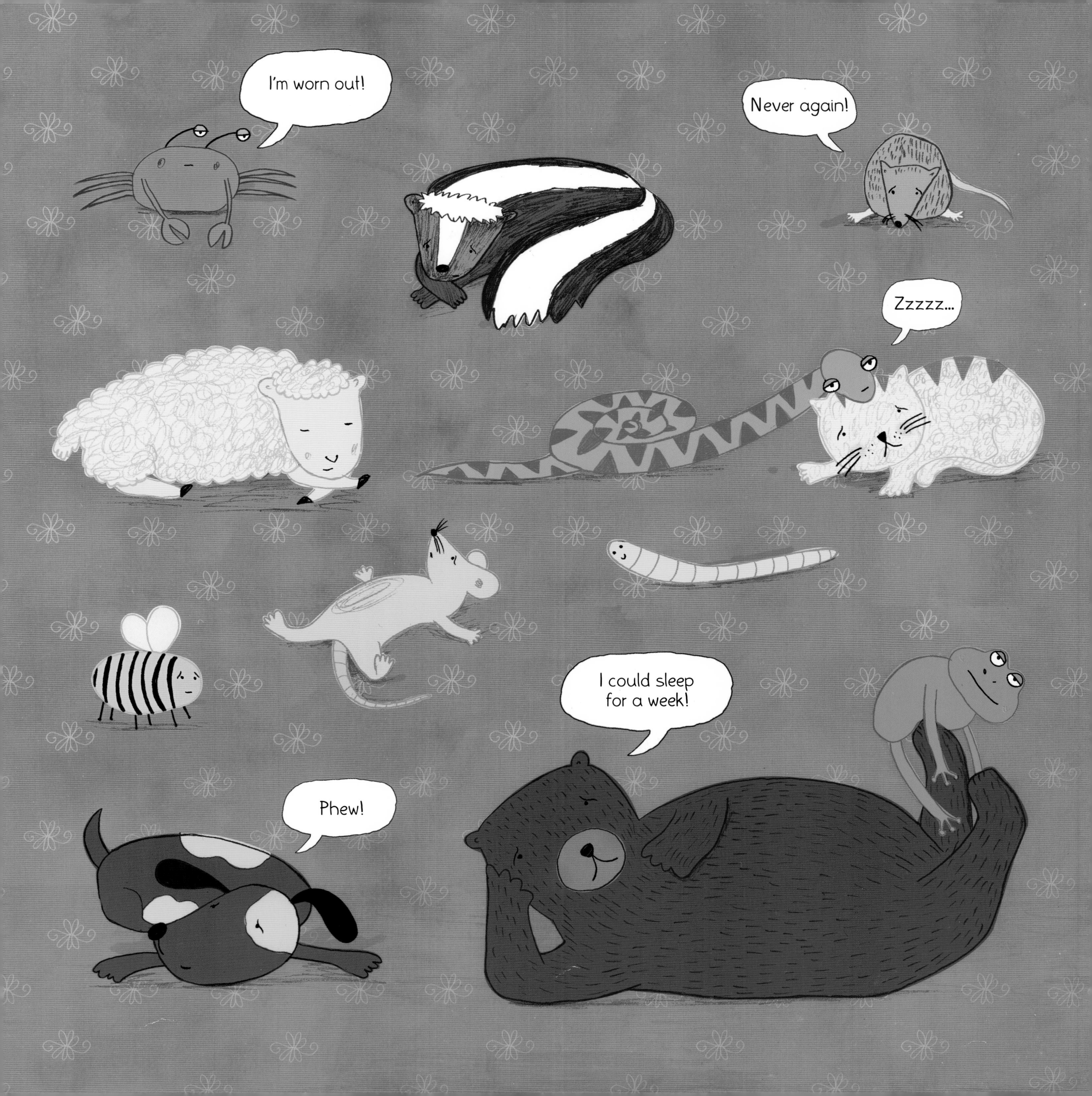
I'm worn out!
Never again!
Zzzzz...
I could sleep for a week!
Phew!